A play by
Gary Soto

PAPERSTAR

A Member of Penguin Putnam Inc.

Professional and amateurs are hereby warned
that this play is subject to a royalty.
For information regarding performance rights,
contact BookStop Literary Agency,
67 Meadow View Road, Orinda, California 94563,
(925)254-2668.

Mil gracias to David Chavez, and
un aplauso to the Drama Club of Sanger High School,
pictured on the cover

Copyright © 1999 by Gary Soto.
All rights reserved. This book, or parts thereof, may not be reproduced
in any form without permission in writing from the publisher.
A PaperStar Book, published in 1999 by Penguin Putnam Books
for Young Readers, 345 Hudson Street, New York, NY 10014.
PaperStar is a registered trademark of The Putnam Berkley Group,Inc.
The PaperStar logo is a trademark of The Putnam Berkley Group, Inc.
Published simultaneously in Canada. Printed in the United States of America.

Library of Congress Cataloging-in-Publication Data
Soto, Gary.   Nerdlandia : a play / Gary Soto.   p.   cm.
Summary: A humorous play in which Martin, a Chicano nerd, undergoes
a transformation with the help of his friends and experiences true love.
Includes a glossary of Spanish words and phrases used in the dialogue.
1. Mexican American youth—Juvenile drama. 2. Young adult drama, American.
[1. Mexican Americans—Drama. 2. Plays.]   I. Title.
PS3569.O72N47   1999   812'.54—dc21   98-37093   CIP   AC
ISBN 0-698-11784-0
10   9   8   7   6   5   4   3   2

Performance Notes

1. Until Scene 4, Martin should mispronounce the Spanish words and phrases. After his heart transplant, his Spanish should be spoken with a correct accent. At that point, the director has the choice of accenting his name, from Martin to Martín. Change in name pronunciation is optional.

2. The play takes place in Fresno, California, but references to towns, schools, restaurants, famous people, etc., may be changed for local appeal.

3. All music should be uncopyrighted, original, or within the public domain.

A glossary of Spanish words and slang begins on page 86.

Characters

Martin, nerdish boy

Joaquin, *vato loco*

Freddie and **Tito**, humorous *vatos locos*

Ceci, love-struck *chola*

Lupe and **Susana**, *cholas*

Scene 1

In front of a high school.

(Eyes downcast, Martin, a Chicano nerd, paces. He sports a calculator on his belt, eyeglasses, white shirt with a thin tie, pants hiked up around his chest. He stops when he sees Joaquin, a cholo wannabe who is "tagging" a wall. Joaquin notices Martin.)

Joaquin: Hey, Martin. How come you're making *la jeta*?

(Not wanting to talk, Martin turns away. Joaquin follows him.)

Joaquin: Come on. What's wrong, homes?

Martin: Nothing's wrong. I'm happy.

Joaquin: You ain't happy. What's up with you? *Qué pasó?*

Martin: Really, I'm fine.

(Joaquin sizes up Martin's sadness.)

Joaquin: Let me guess. You didn't make the football team? Is that it?

Martin: *(in a squeaky voice)* No, I didn't go out for football.

Joaquin: It's a joke, *ese.* I know you didn't go out for the team. If you had, *pues*, we wouldn't be 0–7. More like 0–100. *(pause)* I got it! You broke your microscope?

(Martin wags his head no.)

Joaquin: Your ant farm got sprayed with Black Flag?

Martin: No, my ant farm is just fine. And so is my goldfish and my hamster.

(Joaquin ponders Martin's reluctance to talk.)

Joaquin: Ever since you and me first met in kindergarten—and I was there two years getting my colors down real good—you been into this science stuff. I used to think that you were all *tapado*, stuck up. But no, I admit it, I was wrong. You're just a nerd. I figure your kind of people—nerds—and my kind of people—*vatos*—got to come together. *(pause)* I know what's wrong.

Your calculator's broke!

Martin: No, my calculator works just fine. But thank you for asking. *(pause)* If I tell you, you won't laugh?

(Joaquin puts on a straight face.)

Joaquin: Laugh? Laugh at the *vato* who helps me in biology? Who whispers in my ear the answers to algebra? Who fills me with history during finals? So what's going down?

Martin: It's my heart.

Joaquin: *Tu corazón?*

Martin: *(mispronouncing Spanish)* Yes, my *corazón*. Love palpitations.

Joaquin: Love palpitations. That's a hard one to fix. *Tú sabes*, when you fool with your heart, it's delicate. You get inside a person and change things around. But sometimes it's got to be done.

Martin: You know how to repair a broken heart?

Joaquin: *Simón!* I'm the surgeon of all heart surgeons, a specialist when it comes to romance. Shoot, last week I was on the cellular phone with Leonardo DiCaprio [or current heart-throb]. The *vato* was all heartbroken. He was crying because his girl dumped him! Right in front of El Pollo Loco.

Martin: DiCaprio? He was crying?

Joaquin: Like a rain cloud.

(Enter two vatos locos—Freddie and Tito.)

Joaquin: Mira, here come *nuestros carnales*—Freddie *y* Tito.

(They yuk it up; they shake hands in an unusually complicated, thus comical, raza style.)

Freddie: Man, I got carpal tunnel syndrome from these hand shakes. *(to Joaquin)* So what's going down, Joaquin?

Joaquin: Unemployment, crime, *placas*, and Martin's broken heart.

Freddie: Junior Einstein is heartbroken?

Tito: When I saw his long face, I thought his calculator was broke.

Joaquin: That's what I thought, homes.

(They slap palms; they wince in pain from their carpal tunnel syndrome.)

Tito: *(to Joaquin)* Hey, guess what?

Joaquin: *(mocking Tito)* Hey, I don't know.

Tito: Freddie found a part-time job.

Freddie: *(smiling)* Washing dishes in a Chinese restaurant. I'm going to carry on the family tradition.

(Freddie rubs his palms together, as if washing dishes.)

Joaquin: It seems like our *raza* was born to wash dishes. When did you start?

Freddie: I started when I was seven and my mom made me do the forks and spoons.

Joaquin: No, *tonto*, when did you start the job?

Freddie: Oh. I don't start until this other *vato* gets fired. I'm next in line.

Joaquin: But don't take the job right away because I think we got to help Marty.

(Martin walks slowly away.)

Martin: You guys don't have to. I'll recover.

Joaquin: Martin, you always helped us with school, and we—Freddie, Tito, and me—*pues*, we're going to see you through this dark time.

Freddie: That's right! We can't let our homie down.

Tito: You're the future leader of our people ... plus we need the answers for next week's history quiz. *(pause)* Come on, Marty, smile. Don't be so tight. Show a little teeth.

(The three of them smile big to the audience. Martin starts slowly and then follows suit with a large smile.)

Tito: So who's this girl? Maybe I can talk to her and ... ask her out myself!

Freddie: *Mira este chavalo. Sinvergüenza!* Right away he wants to step in all *suave. (pause)* Yeah, where does this girl live?

Joaquin: Allright, you jugheads, don't play with Marty. Can't you see he's all *triste y todo*?

Freddie: *Triste.*

Tito: *Triste y todo.*

Martin: Just because I'm a nerd, you're making fun of me. But I have feelings too. I like girls just like you three . . . *vatos*.

Joaquin: Of course you do. Nerds got feelings like the rest of us. In fact, you're the most *suavecito* with a 4.0 at school.

Martin: You're just saying that.

Freddie: It's the truth. Your name is always coming up like pimples.

Martin: They just want me to help them with their homework.

Freddie: Nah, homes! They admire you and your intelligence. In fact, I was kicking down the hallway looking for a free sandwich when I heard Belinda Sanchez say in a low, kitty cat voice, "Martin, what a smooth calculator."

Joaquin: *Híjole*, Belinda can turn on the charm.

Tito: *De veras*! She was panting over that big digital machine on your belt.

Martin: I really appreciate that, *mi carnal*. But I know I'm not a *suavecito*. I'm just another Chicano nerd in America. *(pause)* Can I confide in you three?

(The three vatos look at each other.)

Freddie: Confide? Is that anything like *con safos*?

Tito: Sounds like a cussword. Are you calling us a bad word in nerd language? Because we don't take that, *ese*.

Martin: It means, can I tell you something . . . personal?

(All of them ad-lib, "Yeah, go ahead; let it spill, órale," etc.)

Martin: I was listening to this song yesterday while I was filling my petri dish with bacteria, and *(becoming shy)* . . .

Joaquin: *Y qué?*

Martin: I had a strange sensation that the song was exclusively meant for me.

Joaquin: Songs do that, *qué no*? They bring up all these dark emotions. You get your ride, bump along Blackstone Avenue [or local street], the radio up, the girls eyeing you behind big old layers of mascara. *Híjole*, it's the best experience. What song was you listening to, little Marty?

Martin: I appreciate your asking, *carnal*. I don't recall the title, but it went something like this . . .

(Martin sings in a Frank Sinatra-like croon.)

Martin: *(continuing)* Molecules, fluctuating molecules,/floating in the calculus of our feelings./Molecules, fluctuating molecules/drifting in the strata molecular bonding,/I light you like a Bunsen burner,/study you under the microscope of life,/dissect you like a frog,/my barium chromate, my future wife.

(The three stand shocked by Martin's science-laden song.)

Joaquin: I don't know what that was about, *pero* if it moves you, that's good. Come on, jugheads. Give it up! *Aplauso!* *(pause)* So who's this girl anyhow?

Martin: I can't part with her name. My lips are sealed until the rivers run dry and stars go out like lightbulbs.

Freddie: Stop with the poetry, Junior Einstein.

(Martin mutters her name under his breath. The three of them shout that they can't hear him.)

Martin: *(loudly)* Ceci Cortez!

(Joaquin, Freddie, and Tito, shocked and looking in the direction of the audience, yell out, "Ceci Cortez!")

Joaquin: Ceci, that wild heartbreaker? The best-looking girl in our corner of the planet.

Freddie: *Fíjate*, Marty. We got experience with ordinary girls, but good-looking ones, *pues*, we don't know a lot.

Joaquin: Freddie's right. We're all stupid when it comes to items like Ceci.

Freddie: Plus her old man, Sleepy. He would tear us up if he found us trying to set you up with Ceci.

Tito: That's right. We ain't going to mess with Sleepy's girl.

Joaquin: Sleepy ain't nowhere. I'll get my homies to do some of this.

(Freddie and Tito throw a few boxing jabs.)

Joaquin: And some of this.

(Freddie and Tito karate-kick.)

Joaquin: And some of these bad karate chops.

(Freddie and Tito chop the air.)

Joaquin: I would lay him out like a Tortilla—flat.

(Offstage, Sleepy's voice rumbles, "No one better mess with my girl." The three vatos—Joaquin, Freddie, and Tito—huddle together in fear.)

Freddie: Joaquin, you better rethink the game plan. *(pause)* I remember when Sleepy grabbed me by the throat.

Tito: I remember. You had just got a drink of water at the playground. He took you by your throat like a burrito and the *agua* squirted all out.

(Tito pantomimes water leaping from his mouth.)

Joaquin: You're probably right. Sleepy's pretty scary.

Martin: You mean you won't help?

(The boys, sizing up Martin's pathetic situation, moan, "Of course we'll try, homes; sure, why not; órale, we'll stand by you," etc.)

11

Joaquin: You really got the microscope on her, Junior Einstein?

Martin: I think about her all the time. Yesterday when I was plotting the equation to the hyperbola of X minus two times the quantity of the radius of pi, I just floated off into space.

Joaquin: That's pretty heavy. But instead of Ceci, maybe Julieta or Laura or Ana or maybe the new girl from El Salvador. The one that pushes the little *paleta* cart on Saturdays.

Martin: No, my *corazón* is set on Ceci. I dream about her and I even . . .

Joaquin: Even what?

Martin: Hug my pillow.

Joaquin: *Chihuahua!* You got it serious, homeboy. Are you kissing the pillow *también?*

(Martin nods his head yes.)

Freddie: *(pointing offstage)* Hey, look who's coming!

Joaquin: Let's hide.

(Martin, Freddie, and Joaquin hide. Ceci, Susana, and Lupe enter stage. The three girls walk across the stage

with attitude; Lupe sniffs the air.)

Lupe: You smell something?

Ceci: *(sniffing the air)* Boys. *(sniffing the air a second time)* Three, no, four boys.

Susana: *(excited)* Ooooooh. And I thought we were just going over to the library to study.

Ceci: We are. So forget them. Dudes are nothing but trouble.

(The girls leave, and the boys once again show themselves.)

Martin: How come we had to hide?

Joaquin: Practice. We got to practice hiding from girls. Like ninjas. In the future, they'll be all over us.

Freddie: Girls will be all over us?

(Joaquin pats Freddie's shoulder.)

Joaquin: Well, some of us, Freddie. Not all of us.

(Tito looks offstage where the girls had walked off.)

Tito: Yeah, I known Ceci since she was real little. In fact . . . *(stops)*

Freddie: *Qué?* Spill it!

Tito: I can't tell you guys.

Joaquin: *Chale.* We're your homies!

Freddie: *(imitating) Chale.* We're your homies!

(Joaquin gives him a look of "be quiet!")

Joaquin: Your problem is our problem. Unless it means that we might get beat up. Then you're on your own.

Tito: *(babyish)* She stole my bike with trainer wheels, beat me up and . . .

Joaquin: Let it out. It's not good to keep these repressed emotions.

Tito: *(sniveling)* And Ceci called me a bad word.

(Joaquin and Freddie let out a small laugh.)

Tito: It's not funny.

Joaquin: That's right. It's not funny. A girl who steals your trainer-wheel bike will scar you for life.

Freddie: What did Ceci call you?

Tito: I can't tell you.

Joaquin: What do you mean you can't tell us? We've known each other since we were in Pampers—little *vatos locos* kicking up trouble in our strollers.

(The three of them wait for Tito to speak.)

Tito: *(with pretend tears)* She called me the 'c' word.

Joaquin: The 'c' word?

Tito: She called me a . . . *caca.*

Freddie: That's cold!

Joaquin: *Ay*, Tito, don't take it hard. Chin up. Be a Marine. What you suffered is in the past. Look at Marty here. He's hurting big-time right now.

Martin: It's true, Tito. I'm hurting here right in my *corazón.*

Tito: Thanks, Junior Einstein. You and me understand how cruel Ceci can be.

(Offstage, Sleepy's voice rumbles, "You better leave my girl alone.")

15

Martin: *(to offstage voice)* But Sleepy, I love her. Let me show you how. *(singing)* "Molecules, fluctuating molecules—"

(Freddie cuts him off.)

Freddie: No, Marty. You'll just make Sleepy mad singing a song to his girl.

(The four pace, thinking of their precarious situation.)

Joaquin: *Pues*, we're going to rebuild your body. Drop a new heart in you.

Tito: Like a new engine block?

Joaquin: That's right. Like a new engine.

Freddie: We'll get a bucket of Bondo and fill you in, especially that hollow chest of yours.

Tito: Bondo's cool, huh?

Freddie: Yeah. It reminds me of my years at the playground when I used to work with Play-Doh. Squeezing the stuff between your *dedos* like *masa*, making little ashtrays, little Virgin Lupes, statues of Power Rangers, these bad-looking lowriders.

Tito: Remember we used to make plaster-of-paris masks?

Freddie: And yours was so ugly it made babies cry.

Tito: *(proudly)* Yeah, my mask was ugly, huh?

Freddie: *Muy* ugly. Ah, the good old days at the playground.

Joaquin: Listen, the way I figure, instead of the heart transplant, we go simple.

Tito: Simple! We're good at being simple.

(Freddie and Tito slap palms.)

Joaquin: We'll set Marty up with some tough-looking *garras*.

Freddie: Khakis and a Pendleton.

Tito: Like work on the outer self first, huh?

Joaquin: That's it, homes, the outer self. Then if that don't work, we'll work on the inner self. *(pause)* You know, we should trip down to La Raza Mall.

Tito: I heard of the place. They got that restaurant called Tacos-R-Us.

Joaquin: And *una tienda que se llama* Big y Huango.

Freddie: Plus the pawn shop You Snooze You Lose.

Joaquin: *(to Martin)* You ready to check this place out?

Martin: I'll do anything to become a *suavecito*.

Joaquin: OK, then, *vámonos*. Let's get out of here.

(The four leave. Lights dim, then darken.)

Scene 2

In front of the high school.

(Lights come up immediately. Enter Ceci, Lupe, and Susana.)

Susana: Girl, what's wrong with you? I mean, he wears a calculator on his belt!

Lupe: And his *pantalones* are all the way up to his throat. Like they're choking him or something.

Susana: And did you hear what he wants to start? *(Ceci shakes her head)* A club for people into ant farms.

Lupe: *Qué loco!* He's a funny dude.

Ceci: But he's sweet.

Lupe: So! If you want something sweet, buy a soda.

Ceci: I'm not talking thirst, girl. I'm talking about a guy I can trust. He's better than that no-good Sleepy. He said he was going to the library.

Lupe: *(eyeing Susana)* Instead he was with you know who.

Ceci: *(angrily at Susana)* Yeah—her! Susana!

Susana: I'm sorry. He said that you and him broke up. I didn't know. Honest, Ceci. I'm not the kind of *chola* who goes out with her best friend's dude.

Lupe: *La flaca's* telling the truth. She was really sorry, Ceci. She cried exactly ninety-six *lágrimas*. Huh, Susana?

Susana: It's true. I spilled them tears all over my bedroom. And I felt so bad that I let Lupe pull my hair for an hour.

Lupe: *De veras.* I punished that girl.

Ceci: *(tenderly)* I know. I don't mean to be hard. But it still hurts. *(pause)* I was a fool to trust that *ratón* Sleepy. And now look at him. In juvie for putting his name in wet cement. How stupid!

(Offstage, Sleepy's voice rumbles, "You better not go out with Junior Einstein.")

Ceci: *(to offstage voice)* You can't tell me what to

do. We're through, Sleepy. You're locked away and out of my life.

(The girls pace.)

Lupe: It's like the bad experience I had last year.

Ceci: Sleepy hit on you too?

(Lupe grows silent. She walks away from her friends.)

Ceci: What? What happened?

Lupe: Remember when I was in love with Little Ray? And I begged him to let me wear his Raiders jacket?

Ceci: *(frustrated)* Do you have to bring this up again?

Lupe: And I lost it, his jacket. The one his mother had bought him when she won a hundred *bolas* from the lottery. He made me feel so low!

Susana: *Cállate* already.

Lupe: *(with tears)* Then I found it under the bleachers. The jacket his mom bought!

Susana: Get over it, girl.

Lupe: It was all dirty and messed up.

Ceci: Put it behind you! That was last year, not yesterday.

Lupe: *(sniffling)* Alright. I won't talk about it anymore. It's gone. It belongs to the past. We must look toward the future. *(pause)* Then he made me pay for the cleaning bill and told all his friends about it.

Susana: *Ay, Dios.* Every time we talk about romance, you bring up Little Ray and his stupid Raiders jacket.

Ceci: *Vatos* are cruel.

Susana: *Malos* two-timers.

Lupe: Low-down *ratones*.

Susana: *Huevones* to the ninth degree!

(The girls start, one by one, to look out into the audience, noticing the boys.)

Ceci: *Espérate.* Wait a second. Let's not be hasty. *(pointing at a boy)* That one *allá*. He's *fino*.

Susana: *(pointing at another boy)* He's fine too. That *ratoncito* in the front row.

Ceci: *Y el güero* over there. I like your eyes, my little *empanada*.

Lupe: Wait a second. We're getting sidetracked. Guys will do that, make us forget about what's really important.

(Offstage, Sleepy's voice rumbles, "You better not go out with Junior Einstein.")

Ceci: *(to offstage voice) Cállate*! I'll do what I want. You don't own me or nothing. *(to girls)* He thinks I should do what he wants. Forget him!

Susana: Maybe you're right, Ceci. What you need is a guy who is faithful.

Lupe: Kind!

Susana: Intelligent!

Ceci: I like that. A guy who is kind, faithful, and smart. And looks shouldn't matter that much. Even if he's got braces on his teeth.

Susana: I remember this girl telling me that she was making out with this guy with braces.

Lupe: So?

Susana: Braces with these rubber bands. And

when he and the girl were making out, one of his rubber bands shot in her mouth.

Lupe: *Asco!*

(The girls pace.)

Ceci: Looks help, I agree. But for me, personally, I want a guy I can trust.

(Offstage, Sleepy's voice rumbles, "You can trust me, *chola.*")

Ceci: *(to offstage voice)* Shut up, I said!

Lupe: Dudes, they're always promising things.

Susana: That's right. They promise to write love letters, but do they write them? *Mentirosos!* I remember this guy from Kerman [or local town]. We danced and danced and got pretty close in the parking lot. Julio was, *chihuahua*, one hot *tamal.*

Lupe: I think I went out with that guy. He's got a ponytail, no?

Susana: *(eagerly)* And a cute little scar on his chin?

Lupe: And these cowboy boots?

24

A play by
Gary Soto

PAPERSTAR

A Member of Penguin Putnam Inc.

Professional and amateurs are hereby warned
that this play is subject to a royalty.
For information regarding performance rights,
contact BookStop Literary Agency,
67 Meadow View Road, Orinda, California 94563,
(925)254-2668.

Mil gracias to David Chavez, and
un aplauso to the Drama Club of Sanger High School,
pictured on the cover

Copyright © 1999 by Gary Soto.
All rights reserved. This book, or parts thereof, may not be reproduced
in any form without permission in writing from the publisher.
A PaperStar Book, published in 1999 by Penguin Putnam Books
for Young Readers, 345 Hudson Street, New York, NY 10014.
PaperStar is a registered trademark of The Putnam Berkley Group,Inc.
The PaperStar logo is a trademark of The Putnam Berkley Group, Inc.
Published simultaneously in Canada. Printed in the United States of America.

Library of Congress Cataloging-in-Publication Data
Soto, Gary. Nerdlandia : a play / Gary Soto. p. cm.
Summary: A humorous play in which Martin, a Chicano nerd, undergoes
a transformation with the help of his friends and experiences true love.
Includes a glossary of Spanish words and phrases used in the dialogue.
1. Mexican American youth—Juvenile drama. 2. Young adult drama, American.
[1. Mexican Americans—Drama. 2. Plays.] I. Title.
PS3569.O72N47 1999 812´.54—dc21 98-37093 CIP AC
ISBN 0-698-11784-0
10 9 8 7 6 5 4 3 2

For the members of Los Lobos—

Steve Berlin
David Hidalgo
Conrad Lozano
Louie Pérez
Cesar Rojas

keep howling

Performance Notes

1. Until Scene 4, Martin should mispronounce the Spanish words and phrases. After his heart transplant, his Spanish should be spoken with a correct accent. At that point, the director has the choice of accenting his name, from Martin to Martín. Change in name pronunciation is optional.

2. The play takes place in Fresno, California, but references to towns, schools, restaurants, famous people, etc., may be changed for local appeal.

3. All music should be uncopyrighted, original, or within the public domain.

A glossary of Spanish words and alang begins on page 86.

Characters

Martin, nerdish boy

Joaquin, *vato loco*

Freddie and **Tito**, humorous *vatos locos*

Ceci, love-struck *chola*

Lupe and **Susana**, *cholas*

Scene 1

In front of a high school.

(Eyes downcast, Martin, a Chicano nerd, paces. He sports a calculator on his belt, eyeglasses, white shirt with a thin tie, pants hiked up around his chest. He stops when he sees Joaquin, a cholo wannabe who is "tagging" a wall. Joaquin notices Martin.)

Joaquin: Hey, Martin. How come you're making *la jeta*?

(Not wanting to talk, Martin turns away. Joaquin follows him.)

Joaquin: Come on. What's wrong, homes?

Martin: Nothing's wrong. I'm happy.

Joaquin: You ain't happy. What's up with you? *Qué pasó?*

Martin: Really, I'm fine.

(Joaquin sizes up Martin's sadness.)

1

Joaquin: Let me guess. You didn't make the football team? Is that it?

Martin: *(in a squeaky voice)* No, I didn't go out for football.

Joaquin: It's a joke, *ese.* I know you didn't go out for the team. If you had, *pues*, we wouldn't be 0-7. More like 0-100. *(pause)* I got it! You broke your microscope?

(Martin wags his head no.)

Joaquin: Your ant farm got sprayed with Black Flag?

Martin: No, my ant farm is just fine. And so is my goldfish and my hamster.

(Joaquin ponders Martin's reluctance to talk.)

Joaquin: Ever since you and me first met in kindergarten—and I was there two years getting my colors down real good—you been into this science stuff. I used to think that you were all *tapado*, stuck up. But no, I admit it, I was wrong. You're just a nerd. I figure your kind of people—nerds—and my kind of people—*vatos*—got to come together. *(pause)* I know what's wrong.

Your calculator's broke!

Martin: No, my calculator works just fine. But thank you for asking. *(pause)* If I tell you, you won't laugh?

(Joaquin puts on a straight face.)

Joaquin: Laugh? Laugh at the *vato* who helps me in biology? Who whispers in my ear the answers to algebra? Who fills me with history during finals? So what's going down?

Martin: It's my heart.

Joaquin: *Tu corazón?*

Martin: *(mispronouncing Spanish)* Yes, my *corazón.* Love palpitations.

Joaquin: Love palpitations. That's a hard one to fix. *Tú sabes,* when you fool with your heart, it's delicate. You get inside a person and change things around. But sometimes it's got to be done.

Martin: You know how to repair a broken heart?

Joaquin: *Simón!* I'm the surgeon of all heart surgeons, a specialist when it comes to romance. Shoot, last week I was on the cellular phone with Leonardo DiCaprio [or current heart-throb]. The *vato* was all heartbroken. He was crying because his girl dumped him! Right in front of El Pollo Loco.

Martin: DiCaprio? He was crying?

Joaquin: Like a rain cloud.

(Enter two vatos locos—Freddie and Tito.)

Joaquin: Mira, here come *nuestros carnales*—Freddie *y* Tito.

(They yuk it up; they shake hands in an unusually complicated, thus comical, raza style.)

Freddie: Man, I got carpal tunnel syndrome from these hand shakes. *(to Joaquin)* So what's going down, Joaquin?

Joaquin: Unemployment, crime, *placas*, and Martin's broken heart.

Freddie: Junior Einstein is heartbroken?

Tito: When I saw his long face, I thought his calculator was broke.

Joaquin: That's what I thought, homes.

(They slap palms; they wince in pain from their carpal tunnel syndrome.)

Tito: *(to Joaquin)* Hey, guess what?

Joaquin: *(mocking Tito)* Hey, I don't know.

Tito: Freddie found a part-time job.

Freddie: *(smiling)* Washing dishes in a Chinese restaurant. I'm going to carry on the family tradition.

(Freddie rubs his palms together, as if washing dishes.)

Joaquin: It seems like our *raza* was born to wash dishes. When did you start?

Freddie: I started when I was seven and my mom made me do the forks and spoons.

Joaquin: No, *tonto*, when did you start the job?

Freddie: Oh. I don't start until this other *vato* gets fired. I'm next in line.

Joaquin: But don't take the job right away because I think we got to help Marty.

(Martin walks slowly away.)

Martin: You guys don't have to. I'll recover.

Joaquin: Martin, you always helped us with school, and we—Freddie, Tito, and me—*pues*, we're going to see you through this dark time.

Freddie: That's right! We can't let our homie down.

Tito: You're the future leader of our people . . . plus we need the answers for next week's history quiz. *(pause)* Come on, Marty, smile. Don't be so tight. Show a little teeth.

(The three of them smile big to the audience. Martin starts slowly and then follows suit with a large smile.)

Tito: So who's this girl? Maybe I can talk to her and . . . ask her out myself!

Freddie: *Mira este chavalo. Sinvergüenza!* Right away he wants to step in all *suave. (pause)* Yeah, where does this girl live?

Joaquin: Allright, you jugheads, don't play with Marty. Can't you see he's all *triste y todo?*

Freddie: *Triste.*

Tito: *Triste y todo.*

6

Martin: Just because I'm a nerd, you're making fun of me. But I have feelings too. I like girls just like you three . . . *vatos*.

Joaquin: Of course you do. Nerds got feelings like the rest of us. In fact, you're the most *suavecito* with a 4.0 at school.

Martin: You're just saying that.

Freddie: It's the truth. Your name is always coming up like pimples.

Martin: They just want me to help them with their homework.

Freddie: Nah, homes! They admire you and your intelligence. In fact, I was kicking down the hallway looking for a free sandwich when I heard Belinda Sanchez say in a low, kitty cat voice, "Martin, what a smooth calculator."

Joaquin: *Híjole*, Belinda can turn on the charm.

Tito: *De veras*! She was panting over that big digital machine on your belt.

Martin: I really appreciate that, *mi carnal*. But I know I'm not a *suavecito*. I'm just another Chicano nerd in America. *(pause)* Can I confide in you three?

(The three vatos *look at each other.)*

Freddie: Confide? Is that anything like *con safos*?

Tito: Sounds like a cussword. Are you calling us a bad word in nerd language? Because we don't take that, *ese*.

Martin: It means, can I tell you something . . . personal?

(All of them ad-lib, "Yeah, go ahead; let it spill, órale," etc.)

Martin: I was listening to this song yesterday while I was filling my petri dish with bacteria, and *(becoming shy)* . . .

Joaquin: *Y qué?*

Martin: I had a strange sensation that the song was exclusively meant for me.

Joaquin: Songs do that, *qué no?* They bring up all these dark emotions. You get your ride, bump along Blackstone Avenue [or local street], the radio up, the girls eyeing you behind big old layers of mascara. *Híjole*, it's the best experience. What song was you listening to, little Marty?

Martin: I appreciate your asking, *carnal*. I don't recall the title, but it went something like this . . .

(Martin sings in a Frank Sinatra-like croon.)

Martin: *(continuing)* Molecules, fluctuating molecules,/floating in the calculus of our feelings./Molecules, fluctuating molecules/drifting in the strata molecular bonding,/I light you like a Bunsen burner,/study you under the microscope of life,/dissect you like a frog,/my barium chromate, my future wife.

(The three stand shocked by Martin's science-laden song.)

Joaquin: I don't know what that was about, *pero* if it moves you, that's good. Come on, jugheads. Give it up! *Aplauso!* *(pause)* So who's this girl anyhow?

Martin: I can't part with her name. My lips are sealed until the rivers run dry and stars go out like lightbulbs.

Freddie: Stop with the poetry, Junior Einstein.

(Martin mutters her name under his breath. The three of them shout that they can't hear him.)

Martin: *(loudly)* Ceci Cortez!

(Joaquin, Freddie, and Tito, shocked and looking in the direction of the audience, yell out, "Ceci Cortez!")

Joaquin: Ceci, that wild heartbreaker? The best-looking girl in our corner of the planet.

Freddie: *Fíjate*, Marty. We got experience with ordinary girls, but good-looking ones, *pues*, we don't know a lot.

Joaquin: Freddie's right. We're all stupid when it comes to items like Ceci.

Freddie: Plus her old man, Sleepy. He would tear us up if he found us trying to set you up with Ceci.

Tito: That's right. We ain't going to mess with Sleepy's girl.

Joaquin: Sleepy ain't nowhere. I'll get my homies to do some of this.

(Freddie and Tito throw a few boxing jabs.)

Joaquin: And some of this.

(Freddie and Tito karate-kick.)

10

Joaquin: And some of these bad karate chops.

(Freddie and Tito chop the air.)

Joaquin: I would lay him out like a Tortilla—flat.

(Offstage, Sleepy's voice rumbles, "No one better mess with my girl." The three vatos*—Joaquin, Freddie, and Tito—huddle together in fear.)*

Freddie: Joaquin, you better rethink the game plan. *(pause)* I remember when Sleepy grabbed me by the throat.

Tito: I remember. You had just got a drink of water at the playground. He took you by your throat like a burrito and the *agua* squirted all out.

(Tito pantomimes water leaping from his mouth.)

Joaquin: You're probably right. Sleepy's pretty scary.

Martin: You mean you won't help?

(The boys, sizing up Martin's pathetic situation, moan, "Of course we'll try, homes; sure, why not; órale, we'll stand by you," etc.)

Joaquin: You really got the microscope on her, Junior Einstein?

Martin: I think about her all the time. Yesterday when I was plotting the equation to the hyperbola of X minus two times the quantity of the radius of pi, I just floated off into space.

Joaquin: That's pretty heavy. But instead of Ceci, maybe Julieta or Laura or Ana or maybe the new girl from El Salvador. The one that pushes the little *paleta* cart on Saturdays.

Martin: No, my *corazón* is set on Ceci. I dream about her and I even . . .

Joaquin: Even what?

Martin: Hug my pillow.

Joaquin: *Chihuahua!* You got it serious, homeboy. Are you kissing the pillow *también*?

(Martin nods his head yes.)

Freddie: *(pointing offstage)* Hey, look who's coming!

Joaquin: Let's hide.

(Martin, Freddie, and Joaquin hide. Ceci, Susana, and Lupe enter stage. The three girls walk across the stage

with attitude; Lupe sniffs the air.)

Lupe: You smell something?

Ceci: *(sniffing the air)* Boys. *(sniffing the air a second time)* Three, no, four boys.

Susana: *(excited)* Oooooh. And I thought we were just going over to the library to study.

Ceci: We are. So forget them. Dudes are nothing but trouble.

(The girls leave, and the boys once again show themselves.)

Martin: How come we had to hide?

Joaquin: Practice. We got to practice hiding from girls. Like ninjas. In the future, they'll be all over us.

Freddie: Girls will be all over us?

(Joaquin pats Freddie's shoulder.)

Joaquin: Well, some of us, Freddie. Not all of us.

(Tito looks offstage where the girls had walked off.)

Tito: Yeah, I known Ceci since she was real little. In fact . . . *(stops)*

Freddie: *Qué?* Spill it!

Tito: I can't tell you guys.

Joaquin: *Chale.* We're your homies!

Freddie: *(imitating) Chale.* We're your homies!

(Joaquin gives him a look of "be quiet!")

Joaquin: Your problem is our problem. Unless it means that we might get beat up. Then you're on your own.

Tito: *(babyish)* She stole my bike with trainer wheels, beat me up and . . .

Joaquin: Let it out. It's not good to keep these repressed emotions.

Tito: *(sniveling)* And Ceci called me a bad word.

(Joaquin and Freddie let out a small laugh.)

Tito: It's not funny.

Joaquin: That's right. It's not funny. A girl who steals your trainer-wheel bike will scar you for life.

Freddie: What did Ceci call you?

Tito: I can't tell you.

Joaquin: What do you mean you can't tell us? We've known each other since we were in Pampers—little *vatos locos* kicking up trouble in our strollers.

(The three of them wait for Tito to speak.)

Tito: *(with pretend tears)* She called me the 'c' word.

Joaquin: The 'c' word?

Tito: She called me a . . . *caca.*

Freddie: That's cold!

Joaquin: *Ay*, Tito, don't take it hard. Chin up. Be a Marine. What you suffered is in the past. Look at Marty here. He's hurting big-time right now.

Martin: It's true, Tito. I'm hurting here right in my *corazón*.

Tito: Thanks, Junior Einstein. You and me understand how cruel Ceci can be.

(Offstage, Sleepy's voice rumbles, "You better leave my girl alone.")

15

Martin: *(to offstage voice)* But Sleepy, I love her. Let me show you how. *(singing)* "Molecules, fluctuating molecules—"

(Freddie cuts him off.)

Freddie: No, Marty. You'll just make Sleepy mad singing a song to his girl.

(The four pace, thinking of their precarious situation.)

Joaquin: *Pues*, we're going to rebuild your body. Drop a new heart in you.

Tito: Like a new engine block?

Joaquin: That's right. Like a new engine.

Freddie: We'll get a bucket of Bondo and fill you in, especially that hollow chest of yours.

Tito: Bondo's cool, huh?

Freddie: Yeah. It reminds me of my years at the playground when I used to work with Play-Doh. Squeezing the stuff between your *dedos* like *masa*, making little ashtrays, little Virgin Lupes, statues of Power Rangers, these bad-looking lowriders.

16

Tito: Remember we used to make plaster-of-paris masks?

Freddie: And yours was so ugly it made babies cry.

Tito: *(proudly)* Yeah, my mask was ugly, huh?

Freddie: *Muy* ugly. Ah, the good old days at the playground.

Joaquin: Listen, the way I figure, instead of the heart transplant, we go simple.

Tito: Simple! We're good at being simple.

(Freddie and Tito slap palms.)

Joaquin: We'll set Marty up with some tough-looking *garras*.

Freddie: Khakis and a Pendleton.

Tito: Like work on the outer self first, huh?

Joaquin: That's it, homes, the outer self. Then if that don't work, we'll work on the inner self. *(pause)* You know, we should trip down to La Raza Mall.

Tito: I heard of the place. They got that restaurant called Tacos-R-Us.

Joaquin: And *una tienda que se llama* Big y Huango.

Freddie: Plus the pawn shop You Snooze You Lose.

Joaquin: *(to Martin)* You ready to check this place out?

Martin: I'll do anything to become a *suavecito*.

Joaquin: OK, then, *vámonos*. Let's get out of here.

(The four leave. Lights dim, then darken.)

Scene 2

In front of the high school.

(Lights come up immediately. Enter Ceci, Lupe, and Susana.)

Susana: Girl, what's wrong with you? I mean, he wears a calculator on his belt!

Lupe: And his *pantalones* are all the way up to his throat. Like they're choking him or something.

Susana: And did you hear what he wants to start? *(Ceci shakes her head)* A club for people into ant farms.

Lupe: *Qué loco!* He's a funny dude.

Ceci: But he's sweet.

Lupe: So! If you want something sweet, buy a soda.

Ceci: I'm not talking thirst, girl. I'm talking about a guy I can trust. He's better than that no-good Sleepy. He said he was going to the library.

Lupe: *(eyeing Susana)* Instead he was with you know who.

Ceci: *(angrily at Susana)* Yeah—her! Susana!

Susana: I'm sorry. He said that you and him broke up. I didn't know. Honest, Ceci. I'm not the kind of *chola* who goes out with her best friend's dude.

Lupe: *La flaca's* telling the truth. She was really sorry, Ceci. She cried exactly ninety-six *lágrimas.* Huh, Susana?

Susana: It's true. I spilled them tears all over my bedroom. And I felt so bad that I let Lupe pull my hair for an hour.

Lupe: *De veras.* I punished that girl.

Ceci: *(tenderly)* I know. I don't mean to be hard. But it still hurts. *(pause)* I was a fool to trust that *ratón* Sleepy. And now look at him. In juvie for putting his name in wet cement. How stupid!

(Offstage, Sleepy's voice rumbles, "You better not go out with Junior Einstein.")

Ceci: *(to offstage voice)* You can't tell me what to

do. We're through, Sleepy. You're locked away and out of my life.

(The girls pace.)

Lupe: It's like the bad experience I had last year.

Ceci: Sleepy hit on you too?

(Lupe grows silent. She walks away from her friends.)

Ceci: What? What happened?

Lupe: Remember when I was in love with Little Ray? And I begged him to let me wear his Raiders jacket?

Ceci: *(frustrated)* Do you have to bring this up again?

Lupe: And I lost it, his jacket. The one his mother had bought him when she won a hundred *bolas* from the lottery. He made me feel so low!

Susana: *Cállate* already.

Lupe: *(with tears)* Then I found it under the bleachers. The jacket his mom bought!

Susana: Get over it, girl.

Lupe: It was all dirty and messed up.

Ceci: Put it behind you! That was last year, not yesterday.

Lupe: *(sniffling)* Alright. I won't talk about it anymore. It's gone. It belongs to the past. We must look toward the future. *(pause)* Then he made me pay for the cleaning bill and told all his friends about it.

Susana: *Ay, Dios.* Every time we talk about romance, you bring up Little Ray and his stupid Raiders jacket.

Ceci: *Vatos* are cruel.

Susana: *Malos* two-timers.

Lupe: Low-down *ratones.*

Susana: *Huevones* to the ninth degree!

(The girls start, one by one, to look out into the audience, noticing the boys.)

Ceci: *Espérate.* Wait a second. Let's not be hasty. *(pointing at a boy)* That one *allá.* He's *fino.*

Susana: *(pointing at another boy)* He's fine too. That *ratoncito* in the front row.

Ceci: *Y el güero* over there. I like your eyes, my little *empanada*.

Lupe: Wait a second. We're getting sidetracked. Guys will do that, make us forget about what's really important.

(Offstage, Sleepy's voice rumbles, "You better not go out with Junior Einstein.")

Ceci: *(to offstage voice) Cállate!* I'll do what I want. You don't own me or nothing. *(to girls)* He thinks I should do what he wants. Forget him!

Susana: Maybe you're right, Ceci. What you need is a guy who is faithful.

Lupe: Kind!

Susana: Intelligent!

Ceci: I like that. A guy who is kind, faithful, and smart. And looks shouldn't matter that much. Even if he's got braces on his teeth.

Susana: I remember this girl telling me that she was making out with this guy with braces.

Lupe: So?

Susana: Braces with these rubber bands. And

when he and the girl were making out, one of his rubber bands shot in her mouth.

Lupe: *Asco!*

(The girls pace.)

Ceci: Looks help, I agree. But for me, personally, I want a guy I can trust.

(Offstage, Sleepy's voice rumbles, "You can trust me, *chola*.")

Ceci: *(to offstage voice)* Shut up, I said!

Lupe: Dudes, they're always promising things.

Susana: That's right. They promise to write love letters, but do they write them? *Mentirosos!* I remember this guy from Kerman [or local town]. We danced and danced and got pretty close in the parking lot. Julio was, *chihuahua*, one hot *tamal*.

Lupe: I think I went out with that guy. He's got a ponytail, no?

Susana: *(eagerly)* And a cute little scar on his chin?

Lupe: And these cowboy boots?

24

pretty eyes and let's get down and get married.

Joaquin: That's the head-on–collision approach. *(pause)* To tell you the truth, I ain't had a girl-friend since . . .

(Joaquin ponders the time.)

Joaquin: *(continuing)* . . . since second grade when I was in love with Marta Ramirez.

Freddie: What do you mean you were in love with Marta Ramirez?

Joaquin: You know Marta?

Freddie: Yeah, I know her. She was my girl.

Joaquin: Marta with ponytails and pudgy *rodillas*?

Freddie: Marta was in love with me, *ese*.

Joaquin: *Imposible!*

Freddie: What do you mean impossible? She used to give me a burrito sometimes. That's how much she liked me.

Joaquin: That burrito was mine!

Freddie: Your burrito? The one with all the weenies *y huevos*? Plus a splotch of ketchup?

Joaquin: *Claro*! My mom used to make it for me and packed me a whole herd of animal crackers. *(pause)* Me and Marta would suck on their little *patas*, and talk about finger painting and 3 plus 3, *y todo*.

Freddie: *(stunned)* I can't believe Marta was two-timing me in second grade.

(Depressed, Joaquin and Freddie sit down.)

Joaquin: What a *movida* that girl threw on me. My mom used to fix *mi lonche*. Slaved at the stove. Then instead of eating them, I'd go hungry and give them to her.

Freddie: Marta? You sure it was her?

(Joaquin nods his head. Martin breaks the depressing mood and points to the mailbox.)

Martin: Check out the *placas* on the mailbox. Maybe we can get some advice from our ancestors.

Tito: This mailbox is almost as old as the Bible.

(They huddle around the mailbox.)

Joaquin: *(to Freddie)* Dude, ain't this your dad's name?

Freddie: Yeah, it's *mi papi's placa*, but it ain't my mom's name.

Tito: Your dad was a player, *qué no*?

Joaquin: *Quizás.* *(pause)* Here's all sorts of names. Belinda *con* Ralphie. Sara *con* Julio. Carmen *con* David.

Freddie: Check this out. *Chorizo con huevos*!

(Freddie and Tito slap palms and yuk it up.)

Joaquin: *Mira*! Here's my mom's name. José *con* Patricia.

Tito: I think that "José" is my dad! I recognize his *placa*.

Joaquin: Your dad? Your dad used to like my mom? That's weird, homes. We're almost like brothers. *Hermanos*!

Tito: That's weird alright. And just think. If they had gotten married, we would have never been born. Never existed! This whole Chicano reality would have been nada, *nada*!

Joaquin: I'm glad that my mom dumped your dad.

Martin: *(pointing to another "placa")* This is sound advice. "Don't get fooled by plastic love." *Muy profundo.* Kind of like a Chicano Socrates!

Freddie: *(in a crybaby voice)* That's for sure. Like Marta Ramirez when she gave Joaquin's burrito to me. I feel bad, really low.

Martin: Hold yourself together. Be strong!

Freddie: I'll try. I'm giving us *chucos* a bad name, crying onstage. But it hurts.

Martin: I know it hurts. I've been there.

(Freddie stops crying.)

Martin: That's better.

Tito: *(examining mailbox)* There's all kinds of names. Armando *con* Patricia.

Martin: Patricia *con* Ralphie.

Tito: Ralphie *con* Carolina.

Martin: Carolina *con* Chato. And look at this! Joaquin *con* Susana. Joaquin *con* Susana? *(the three* *look at Joaquin)* Hey, Romeo, are you this Joaquin?

(Joaquin smiles shyly.)

Tito: Look at him smile his *gran gatito* smile. Is this the Susana that's friends with Ceci?

Joaquin: So?

Martin: That's cool. I like Ceci, and you like Susana, and these *vatos* here are left out in the cold.

(Freddie walks toward the audience, chest stuck out.)

Freddie: *Ni modo.* We can can find a girl anytime.

Tito: *(surprised)* We can?

Freddie: *Simón.* We just . . . call one of those 900 numbers. Or . . . *(scanning the audience)* Hey, that little pumpkin *allá*, she's cute.

Tito: And her over there.

Freddie: And this *muchacha* with the wild hair. What's your number, girl?

Martin: That's enough drooling, you dogs. *(pause)* Let's get on with life. Let me buy you guys a soda. You really fixed me up.

Joaquin: You're allright, bro. Let's go.

Martin: Sodas for everyone. Big Gulps with lots of ice!

(They shake hands and all four depart, strutting off the stage. Lights dim as music plays, then darken. Lights come up on Susana and Lupe.)

Lupe: You think there's something wrong with Ceci?

Susana: I don't know. She's sure different, huh? Different from before.

Lupe: When I went to her house, she had a bird feeder, an aquarium, a pet turtle, a butterfly net, and that microscope from the store. She was on her bed and instead of *Lowrider* magazine, she was reading *National Geographic*.

Susana: Ceci has really changed.

Lupe: But you know, maybe she's right about school. We got to study a little more. Maybe we can be nurses.

Susana: Not nurses, doctors!

Lupe: I like that—doctors. We can help our *gente* when they're sick.

Susana: Or maybe we can become veterinarians. Take care of the dogs and cats *en el barrio*.

Lupe: *Claro que sí!* They need help too.

Susana: *(reflecting)* Ceci is just going through a phase in her life. We've got to stick by her.

Lupe: Like peanut butter on a flour *tortilla*. We got to stick!

(Enter Ceci, dressed in a nerdish skirt, with glasses and a calculator. She pushes a cart, which holds a microscope, a chess set, and other scientific props.)

Ceci: *(in mispronounced Spanish)* Hola! Cómo están mis amigas?

(Susana and Lupe look at one another, confused.)

Ceci: How do I look?

Lupe: *(muttering to Susana)* Remember to stick by her. *(to Ceci)* You look really, really . . . different. But good different.

Ceci: I cut my fingernails, too.

Lupe: You didn't! *(examining them)* You did! You had the most beautiful fingernails in *el barrio*.

Susana: Your mascara. It's gone!

Ceci: *Y mi mariposa.*

(She shows her once-tattooed ankle.)

Lupe: You had your tattoo lasered?

Ceci: *(nodding her head)* It's gone. I'm going to snag my nerd. *(from the shopping cart, she brings out item after item)* I got my microscope, my Bunsen burner, my Erlenmeyer flasks, and my chessboard. And I even have a graphing calculator exactly like Martin's!

Lupe: I thought it was kind of big for a pager.

Susana: *(rolling her eyes at Lupe)* I'm sure he'll be impressed.

Ceci: *(taking up two chess pieces)* I'm excited. *(pause)* Did you know that you're not supposed to move your queen until you've made at least three moves? I read it in a book.

(Susana and Lupe yawn at this information.)

Ceci: *(continuing)* And did you know that the queen termite is a thousand times larger than her subjects? *(pause)* Do you think Martin will like me?

Susana: "Like" is not the word. You're a dream come true.

Lupe: Ceci, we're really worried about you. We love you. Why can't you be a homegirl like us no more?

(Ceci looks into the microscope.)

Ceci: If we didn't have the ozone layer in place, cosmic gases could reach earth.

Susana: Sounds *fuchi*.

Lupe: *(to Susana)* We're going to have to do something to bring her back. *(pause)* It's all Sleepy's fault. He treated her like dirt.

Susana: That's for sure.

Lupe: If Ceci goes crazy on us, we'll bring in a *curandera* to help her out.

Susana: Or a priest. Just like when that girl in The Exorcist was twisting her head around and around and acting all weird.

(They twist their heads around.)

Lupe: Stuff like that really happens.

(The boys enter, walking their lowriding strut, aloof to the three girls. They kneel and look tough.)

Martin: *Qué pasa*, homegirls?

Susana: Kicking back. Hanging.

(Martin circles Susana and Lupe.)

Martin: Susana *y* Lupe.

Susana: *(happily)* You know our names?

Martin: Sure. I see you at school.

Lupe: *(flirting)* You go to our school? I don't think I seen you before.

Susana: We would have noticed a pretty face like yours.

(Martin smiles to the audience.)

Martin: Maybe you didn't look hard enough.

Susana: Nah, me and Lupe are always looking. Huh, girl?

Lupe: *Siempre*.

Martin: I was around. You were too busy to

notice. *Soy* Martin Pablo Alvarez Gonzalez de Vaca. But I go by the name of—

(Joaquin steps between them.)

Joaquin: *(to Martin, in a near whisper)* Don't let on who you are. Be calm, *ese*.

(Martin considers the advice.)

Martin: I've been around. I'm what you call a dude with a split personality.

Lupe: That's good. One personality for me and one for Susana.

(Susana and Lupe take hold of Martin's arms, then slowly begin to tug at him. Martin breaks away when Ceci enters. He's struck by Ceci's nerdish beauty. In turn, Ceci is struck by Martin's cholo appearance.)

Ceci: *(nerdishly)* Hi.

(Martin becomes shy.)

Ceci: I said, "Hi." You look remarkably swell!

Martin: *(timidly)* Who, me?

(Martin hides behind Joaquin.)

Joaquin: What's wrong? This ain't the first day of kindergarten. Don't be shy.

Martin: *(to Joaquin)* She's so pretty.

(Joaquin looks her up and down.)

Joaquin: Whatever moves you. If you think she's cute, then get in there. Show her your Chicano magnetism.

Martin: I can't! Look at me. I'm a *cholo* and she's so *(to the audience)* . . . so perfect.

(Lights darken.)

Scene 5

A high school classroom with desks, a globe, a flag, etc. The teacher, a mannequin–like figure, sits behind the desk.

(Lights come up, stage right. Martin, newly made cholo, *skims through a school yearbook.)*

Martin: I can't find her in the yearbook. It's not Gloria. Or Iris. Maybe it's this girl with her eyes closed. I hate it when you take a picture with your eyes like this *(closing eyes)* or sometimes your face is like this . . .

(Martin makes an ugly face at the audience, then returns his attention to the yearbook.)

Martin: *(continuing)* It's not her either. *(slamming the yearbook closed)* I've been in high school for three years. I can't believe I didn't notice her before. She's a real beautiful nerd girl and I'm, *pues*, check me out. A *cholo*. A *cholo* for life.

(Martin pulls at his Pendleton, but it refuses to come off. He's wearing a hairnet and he tugs at it, but it too refuses to come off.)

Martin: *Y mis garras!* They won't come off. I'm stuck in this reality.

(Joaquin, now dressed as a nerd, tiptoes into the classroom, but stops in his tracks. Late for class, he addresses his teacher.)

Joaquin: I'm sorry I'm late, Mrs. Ponce. Stay after school? But I got a good lie, I mean, a good reason. My stupid little brother ate a whole box of crayons. I had to drive him over to emergency. I promise, it won't happen again. *(pause as he listens to his teacher)* Thanks, Mrs. Ponce. I won't let the punk eat crayons again.

(Relieved that he's off the hook, Joaquin takes a seat.)

Martin: *Qué pasó?* What's going on with you?

Joaquin: Nothing.

Martin: What do you mean nothing? How come you're dressed like that?

Joaquin: *(shyly)* I want to be a nerd too.

70

Martin: Get out of here.

Joaquin: *En serio.* I got me an ant farm just like you.

Martin: I'm going to hit you, man.

Joaquin: You know that nerd girl we saw yesterday?

(Martin nods his head.)

Joaquin: I like her a lot.

Martin: What! You can't like her!

(Joaquin gets Martin into a headlock, but lets go to direct his attention to the teacher.)

Joaquin: No, Mrs. Ponce, we ain't fighting. I was searching his head for lice. For *piojos.* They run in his family.

Martin: Yeah, on my dad's side.

(Martin and Joaquin smile at the teacher.)

Martin: You can't like her. I like her!

Joaquin: You got Ceci.

(Martin considers Joaquin's remark.)

Martin: When did this happen?

Joaquin: Last night, in bed. *(hesitant)* Man, I never really had a girlfriend.

Martin: What are you saying?

Joaquin: I said, I never really had a girlfriend. I'm telling you the truth. I put on like I'm all *suave*, all bad, but I ain't! And all the fights I got into, heck, I lost them all.

Martin: *(concerned)* What are you saying?

Joaquin: I'm saying that I think I got a chance with this nerd girl. I thought maybe her ants would like to kick around with my ants. *Tú sabes?*

Martin: *Imposible.* I got my eye on her.

Joaquin: But you're a *cholo.* Anyhow, you wanted Ceci. You got to make up your mind.

(Martin appears downcast.)

Martin: All my life I've been waiting for a girl like her to show up, and finally when she does, *pues*, I'm not her type no more. I'm this other person, and I can't change.

Joaquin: *(referring to the yearbook)* What you got there, homes? I mean, *(nerdishly)* what is that you're perusing so intently?

Martin: The yearbook. She's got to be here.

(Joaquin stares at Martin's hairnet.)

Joaquin: Your hairnet's cool. I been a nerd *(looking at watch)* for only three hours, and I miss being a *cholo. Pero* those days are gone.

(Freddie and Tito enter, tiptoeing.)

Freddie: I'm sorry I'm late, Mrs. Ponce. My *mocoso* brother ate some crayons. I had to take his little *nalgas* down to emergency.

Tito: *(to teacher)* And I had to go with the dude for moral and spiritual support. Nah, we won't be late ever again 'cause Freddie's brother ate the whole box. What, Mrs. Ponce? That was Joaquin's excuse? *(to Joaquin)* Hey, man, you're always stealing our excuses. Get your own— *(becoming aware of Joaquin's clothes)* Why you dressed like that?

(Freddie and Tito are struck by Joaquin's nerdish

attire. They mouth their amazement as lights fade. Lights come up, stage left, on the same classroom configuration of chairs, globe, flag, etc. But hanging behind them is a portrait of Martin as nerd and the caption "Student of the Year." Ceci, Lupe, and Susana are seated, secretly munching on french fries.)

Ceci: *(dreamily)* That new guy! He was one delicious-looking brown item on the menu.

Lupe: Like the best dish on the menu.

Ceci: A hot *tamal.*

Susana: Just like these french fries.

Lupe: *Cómo?*

Susana: Didn't you notice his cool walk? Sort of like this.

(Susana takes two french fries and scissors them like walking legs.)

Ceci: That's cute, Susana. But he's much more impressive than french fries. I was born for him.

Susana: But you have your eye on Martin.

Ceci: *(downcast)* I know I said I liked him. But I liked this other guy too.

Lupe: You can't have them all. Leave some for us. You take Junior Einstein, and me and Susana, we'll fight over this dude.

Susana: The best *chola* wins.

(They shake hands. Ceci stands up and paces.)

Ceci: You're right. Now look at me. I'm caught in this role that I invented for myself. *(to the teacher as she sits back down)* Sorry, Mrs. Sierra. *(pulling at back of skirt)* I had to stand up because I had a wedgie.

Lupe: I knew this would come back on you. Just when you gave up on *vatos locos*, here's one worth keeping.

Ceci: There's something about him. He looks familiar, *qué no?* Like we seen him before?

Lupe: I had that feeling *también*.

(Lupe turns and studies the portrait of Martin as Student of the Year. She gets up from her desk and approaches it.)

Lupe: The new *vato* kind of looks like Martin. Nah, it can't be. *(to the teacher)* Why am I out of my seat? Uh, I'm sraightening the picture. You know how us Rams [or local school mascot] have our school pride.

(Lupe sits back down and leans over Ceci's shoulder, as they flip through the yearbook.)

Ceci: Check the yearbook again. He's got to be in here.

(The bell rings for recess. Lights come up, stage right, where the boys are now standing by their desks. Susana and Lupe walk to the middle of the stage while Ceci hovers in the back among her scientific equipment. Susana and Lupe approach Joaquin, struck by his nerdish attire.)

Susana: *(to Joaquin)* What's with you, homeboy? Did you go to a slumber party at Junior Einstein's house?

(Joaquin turns away, and Martin steps forward.)

Lupe: *(to Susana)* There he is!

(Susana and Lupe take hold of Martin and begin to pull on him. He breaks away.)

Martin: *Cálmate!*

(Martin turns to dust the portrait of himself as Student of the Year.)

Martin: I heard of this dude. Good things *también*.

Lupe: He ain't nowhere. *(pause)* We looked in the yearbook, but we couldn't find you.

Martin: I'm there. Did you check out the science club?

(Susana and Lupe shake their heads.)

Martin: I was invisible to you two, all because I was different. Let me give you a hint.

(He pulls back his Pendleton to display his calculator. The girls are shocked.)

Lupe: Impressive calculator.

Martin: *(closing his Pendleton)* Be cool, girl. There is a time and place for playing with my calculator.

Susana: You can't be. You're not—Martin? The Chicano nerd?

Martin: The former Chicano nerd. I had a heart transplant, but I kept my math skills intact. *(gesturing to Joaquin.) Mis carnales* fixed me all up.

Joaquin: It's true. Took a little Bondo to his *cuerpo, y* presto, you had one of these—

Tito: *(butting in)* Transmissions, huh?

Joaquin: Transformations, *tonto*! How many times do I got to tell you?

(Lupe and Susana flirt outrageously with Martin.)

Lupe: You're looking really good, Martin.

Susana: I saw him first.

Lupe: *Mentirosa*, I did!

(Martin waves off Susana and Lupe.)

Martin: I'm going to be direct. I'm looking for Ceci Cortez, the Little Red Riding Hood *de mi corazón. (downcast)* Also, I got my eye on that pretty nerd girl. She was with you yesterday.

(Ceci steps forward, ready to leap into his arms.)

Lupe: *(eyeing Ceci)* She's busy right now.

Susana: Real busy.

(Martin eyes nerdish Ceci.)

Martin: *(to the audience)* The dilemma. Two types of loves. But here's my one chance. Ceci would be fine, *pero* I'm attracted to this item *también.*

(Martin approaches her slowly, but Joaquin pushes his way between them.)

Joaquin: *(nerdishly, to Ceci)* Hi, cutie!

(Ceci pushes him out of her way.)

Joaquin: *(stomping his foot)* I'm never going to snag a girl.

(Freddie and Tito comfort Joaquin.)

Martin: *(to Ceci)* Girl, you look *muy* familiar.

Ceci: No, I'm just your basic nerd.

Martin: No, there's something special.

(Martin pulls her sweater aside, revealing a calculator.)

Martin: *(continuing)* Cool calculator.

79

Ceci: It's a Texas Instrument, model TI95.

(Martin eyes the shopping cart loaded with scientific equipment.)

Martin: And your chess set, and your micro-scope. *(pause)* You haven't seen this *chola* named Ceci? She called one of my homeboys *(pointing to Tito)* a bad word when they were in second grade.

Tito: *(in a crybaby voice)* She made me cry when she called me a *"caca."* That mean ol' Ceci.

Ceci: No, I haven't met her yet. But I hear she's a really nice girl.

Martin: Yeah, well, I like her, and I, you know, *(muttering)* I like you *también.*

Joaquin: This is sorry. I been a *cholo* all my life and after one day he's getting them all.

Ceci: *(to Martin)* You do? You like me?

Martin: And I like your glasses.

Ceci: You know how to flatter a girl.

Lupe: *(steaming)* Hey, I saw the *vato* first, Ceci!

(Lupe covers her mouth, having let the cat out of the bag. Everyone appears shocked. Martin circles Ceci.)

Martin: Ceci? *(pause)* I used to have a crush on you when I was a Chicano nerd. I used to look in my microscope and I couldn't concentrate on all the bacteria and germs. You were taking over my life, *mi vida.* Then tears would fall from my eyes, ninety-six *lágrimas.*

Ceci: I felt the same, Martin. Sometimes when I was listening to the radio, I pictured you in the songs.

Martin: You liked me back then?

Ceci: I did. And I do now.

(Ceci sings a portion of the nerdish song.)

Ceci: Molecules, fluctuating molecules,/floating in the calculus of our feelings.

Martin: I love that oldie but goodie. *(pause)* We've changed. Look at me, Ceci, and look at yourself. Maybe we could slip out of these *trajes.* We can meet halfway.

Ceci: Here on the stage? People are looking.

81

Martin: *(to the audience)* Close your eyes. No peeking.

(Ceci removes her eyeglasses and steps out of her billowy dress into a sleek aerobic outfit. Martin takes off his Pendleton and fits a tie around his neck. He puts on fashionable eyewear.)

Martin: *(to the audience)* OK, open *sus ojos!* *(to Ceci)* You heard of Romeo and Juliet. They ain't nothing compared to us. We're the real thing.

Susana: That's so romantic.

(Susana leans against Joaquin's shoulder. Freddie and Tito place their heads against each other. They push away after they realize what they're doing.)

Ceci: *(to Joaquin)* Susana saw your name and hers together on the mailbox. It said, "Joaquin *con* Susana."

(Susana jumps away from Joaquin's shoulder.)

Martin: *Adelante!* Go, *tigre.* Tell Susana your feelings.

Joaquin: But I'm dressed *(looking at himself)* like this.

82

Martin: Go for it, dude. Don't let your *garras* keep you back.

(Joaquin walks up to Susana in a low-slow walk.)

Joaquin: *(in a mousey voice)* Hi, cutie pie. *(clearing, then deepening his voice)* Qué pasa, paloma? You looking *muy fina*.

Susana: Why are you dressed like that?

Joaquin: I can't really explain. But I can explain how I feel.

Susana: *Ay, qué macho!* I saw your name on the mailbox. You spelled "eternally" wrong. You sure your feelings are true?

Joaquin: Baby, I'm for real—r-e-e-l.

Susana: That's close enough.

(They sway arm in arm as in a dance)

Tito: What about us? Me and Freddie! We never get nobody!

Lupe: *(beckoning with a finger)* Hey, Freddie. I used to have a crush on your older brother. He's in the Marines, *qué no*?

Freddie: He's a barber in the Marines now. But when I go, I'm going to drive a tank. I'm going to throw my switch and hop my tank.

(He hops his body as he pretends to hit the hydraulics of a lowrider.)

Lupe: *(leaning on his shoulder)* Qué ambition!

(Freddie hurries to the chalkboard and sounds out the words as he writes "Freddie con Lupe.")

Tito: This is sorry. I feel bad. There ain't nobody for me. It's the story *de mi vida*. I never get to write "Tito *con* Gloria" or "Tito *con* Maya" or "Tito *con* Araceli". I didn't even get to say the "*chorizo con huevos*" line.

(The couples begin to dance slowly. Tito pouts.)

Tito: *(continuing)* Everyone's got somebody except me. My mom has my dad, and my dad has his beer and TV. My sister has somebody, and you guys got something sweet happening. Even my dog Humo has a girl dog, a little poodle from down the block. *(scaning the audience)* Espérate! Wait a minute. Hey, there's one out

there for me. *Chihuahua*, I see her. You got a
boyfriend? *Ven acá!* Come here, girl . . .

*(Tito brings a girl up from the audience. He asks her
name and he takes her hand. The couples part. They
sing part of the nerdish song.)*

Together: Molecules, fluctuating molecules,/
floating in the calculus of our feelings.

(Lights dim, then darken.)

END

Selected Spanish, Caló, and brand-name words used in *Nerdlandia*;

Informal definitions:

allá   over there
asco   nauseous feeling
bolas   dollars
Bondo   plasterlike material for filling in car dents
cállate!   be quiet!
cálmate!   calm down!
carnal(es)   brother(s), blood brother(s)
chale   no way
chingasos   punches, as in fighting
chisme   gossip
chones   underwear
chucos   from pachucos; zoot suiters
claro que sí   of course
cochino   dirty
con safos   a sign-off on graffiti; a sort of "amen"
cuento   story
cuerpo   body
cuidado!   careful!
curandera   healer
de veras   truthfully
en serio   seriously
espérate!   wait a minute!

feo   ugly
fíjate!   look here!
flaca   skinny
fuchi   smelly
garras   clothes; rags
gorro   hat
güero   person of light complexion
híjole   oh, wow
huevones   lazy persons
jefe   boss; father
jeta   long face
lágrimas   tears
mariposa   butterfly
mentirosos   liars
mira este chavalo!   look at this boy!
mocoso   snotty person
movida   secret plan
muy lejos   very far
nalgas   butt; fanny
nel   no
ni modo   no way
novio   boyfriend
órale   all right
paleta   popsicle
panadería   bakery
patas   legs
placa   graffiti mark; signature

pleitos   fights
puro pedo   pure nonsense
qué piensas?   what do you think?
qué quibo?   how goes it?
rasqüachi   something in shambles
rodillas   knees
simón   that's right
sinvergüenza   without shame
sustos   bad spirits
tapado   stuck up
tonto   dummy
trajes   clothes
triste   sad
tú sabes   you know
vatos locos   crazy dudes
ven   come on
yo creo   I believe